STEAMTEAM 5: BOOK 1

THE BEGINNING

GREG HELMSTETTER

PAMELA METIVIER

MONSOON PUb.

Be sure to follow this book series on www.STEAMTeam5.com.

Written by Greg Helmstetter & Pamela Metivier

Illustrated by Greg Helmstetter

Printed in the U.S.A.

CONTENTS

OTHER STEAMTEAM 5 BOOKS

STEAMTeam 5 Book 2: Mystery at Makerspace

STEAMTeam 5 Chronicles: Mystery of the Haunted Cider Mill

STEAMTeam 5 Chronicles: Evelyn Engineer and the Lightning Treasure

FREE EBOOK

To receive a free .PDF of *STEAMTeam 5 Chronicles: Mystery of the Haunted Cider Mill*, send an email to info@steamteam5.com.

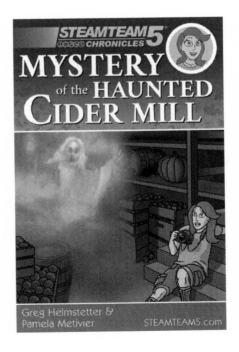

The future belongs to those who believe in the beauty of their dreams.

— Eleanor Roosevelt

When I was a young girl, I made friends with four amazing girls. We became STEAMTeam 5.

Together, we changed the world.

This is how it all began.

Sandia

Sandia Scientist
Valles Marineris Base 2
Mars
June 21, 2055

PART I
ORIGINS

1

SANDIA SCIENTIST

*F*rom the moment Sandia was born, she was curious about the world. She'd spend hours watching something, wondering how it worked.

One day, baby Sandia observed that when she let go of a toy, it dropped to the ground.

When I drop something, it falls to the ground, Baby Sandia thought to herself. As she continued to drop her toys, one by one, they all fell to the ground.

Baby Sandia had formed a hypothesis, which is an explanation for something that you see happen.

One morning, Sandia decided to test her new hypothesis by dropping a handful of applesauce from her high chair. But the applesauce did not fall. It just stuck to her little hand. Sandia looked at her applesauce-covered hand and thought, *Maybe it didn't fall because it's sticky.*

So she formed a new hypothesis: Non-sticky things fall, and sticky things don't fall.

Sandia tested her new hypothesis using a series of experiments—some much messier than others.

"Sandia, my little scientist," her mother grinned, as she cleaned up the piles of goop off the floor.

WHEN SANDIA WAS OLDER, SHE CARRIED A MAGNIFYING GLASS and small jars wherever she went. She collected samples of things she wanted to take a closer look at, such as flowers, rocks, and bugs.

"Check out my new *specimens!*" she'd beam as she emptied her backpack after a successful day of collecting.

One day, while on a hike, Sandia's family came upon a stream. Sandia's mother told her not to drink any water from it. "The water is dirty," her mother warned.

Sandia looked closely at the water. It didn't *look* dirty.

"Hmm. Curious," said Sandia.

She collected some of the water in a jar to take a closer look later.

When Sandia got home, she looked at the specimen she had collected under her microscope.

"Eureka!" shrieked Sandia. The water was not clean at all. It had thousands of tiny creatures in it!

"Those are called microorganisms," her mother explained.

As Sandia grew older, her fascination about the world grew and grew.

Every day, she asked new questions.

Where does the sun go at night?

Where do stars come from?

What makes cheese get moldy?

Why do cats sleep all day?

And every day, she came up with new hypotheses to try to answer her questions.

Then she tested her answers by doing experiments, gathering information, and adding notes to her notebooks.

One afternoon, Sandia spotted something strange while

looking out her bedroom window. A moving truck was parked in front of the house next door. Movers were unloading boxes and furniture from the truck.

"Curious indeed!" Sandia exclaimed.

Sandia watched the house all day, until it got dark.

The movers were finally finishing up when Sandia saw strange flashes of brilliant bluish-white light coming from the new neighbor's backyard. Sandia's mind started thinking up one hypothesis after another to explain these crazy lights.

What could they be? Lightning? Spies? Aliens?

Sandia was determined to find out what caused the flashing lights. So, the next night, she watched again for the lights. Just after sunset, the lights flashed!

Sandia pulled out her notebook and logged the details of what she had just witnessed.

Day 2: Bright lights began flashing at 8:00pm. Repeated at 8:01, 8:02, 8:03, 8:04, 8:05, 8:06, 8:07, 8:08, 8:09 and 8:10.

By the third day of tracking the light activity in her notebook, she noticed a pattern: The lights always came on at the same time every day, an hour after sunset. And they flashed every minute for ten minutes.

"The sky is too clear for it to be lightning, and no good spy would ever behave so predictably, every day," she thought.

"Eureka! It must be aliens!"

Sandia knew that in order to test her alien hypothesis, she'd need to get a closer look. So she got permission to stake out the backyard after dinner.

She set up all of her scientific gear in the backyard and waited.

And waited. And waited.

Suddenly, a brilliant flash of light lit up the backyard and Sandia was startled by a loud scream.

"YEAAAAHHHOOOOOOO!!!!!"

"What was that?!" Sandia gasped to herself. *An alien scream?* she wondered.

But then she thought for a moment...

"That scream sounded almost... human. And if it was a human, then my hypothesis is wrong. I need more information," she realized.

Cautiously, Sandia approached the fence and asked, "Hello? Who's there?"

A face popped up from behind the fence.

"Eureka!" cried Sandia.

"Wh-who are you?" asked Sandia, still a bit nervous. "And what are those bright flashes of light I've been seeing at night?"

"I'm Treeka... short for Teresa. I'm your new neighbor!"

"Oh! You're... human," sighed Sandia. (Sandia had been waiting her whole life to witness aliens.)

But this did not solve the mystery. Sandia still had questions. "What are those bright flashing lights?" she asked.

"I'm looking for bats!" replied Treeka. "Did you know bats live here? So many bats. I love it! They're nocturnal—just like me."

"I've been trying to take a picture of one for days," said Treeka. "And I just got a perfect shot! I was so excited that I screamed."

"Bats?" asked Sandia. "Sweet! How do you photograph them?"

"It's tricky," said Treeka. "They're very fast and zig-zaggy. I kept missing them last night."

"So, tonight, I hooked up a motion detector to my camera —and, voila!"

Treeka peered over Sandia's shoulder into the backyard. "Nice telescope! What do you use it for?"

"Astronomy. It's sort of a hobby of mine," said Sandia. "I use it to look at stars."

"Hmm," Treeka thought, raising one eyebrow (as she did whenever she had an idea).

"I'll bet I could attach *your* telescope to *my* camera!"

"Wow, really?" Sandia responded in excitement. "You mean... we can take pictures... of stars?"

"You bet! I'll just grab my adapter," said Treeka.

WITHIN MINUTES, THEY WERE SNAPPING PHOTOS OF THE Andromeda Galaxy.

"You know what," Sandia said. "My friends and I are having an outdoor slumber party tomorrow night at my friend Mattie's house—she's your neighbor on the other side."

"Oh, I met Mattie earlier today!" Treeka exclaimed. "And she invited me to her slumber party, too!"

"Awesome," Sandia replied. "We're all bringing a surprise to share with the others. No pressure, but feel free to bring something fun or cool," Sandia suggested.

"I know just the thing!" Treeka grinned.

SANDIA AND TREEKA STAYED UP FOR HOURS, LOOKING AT STARS, laughing, and talking about all kinds of exciting new ways they could play together.

2

TREEKA TECHNOLOGIST

*T*reeka's parents were delighted to welcome their first child at 10:10 p.m. on October the tenth.

As an infant, Treeka made it clear that she preferred staying up all night and sleeping most of the day.

Treeka loved to figure things out. In a matter of months, she learned how to release the latch on her crib so she could escape to play with Blue Bear, her talking teddy bear, long into the wee hours. As soon as the sun started to come up, she would climb back into her crib and drift off to sleep.

"I've never seen a baby with its days and nights mixed up like this," her grandmother observed.

"She's quite the enigma," her mother agreed.

"Oh, Teresa is just nocturnal," her father explained.

"Treeka," Treeka chimed in, reminding them of the nickname she had given herself.

Treeka's father worked in his home office most days. Each afternoon, he would take a short break to let baby Treeka sit on his lap so she could play computer games that he created for her.

Her favorite was a game where she used the computer's mouse to match colors and shapes. By the time she was two years old, she was able to make her own shapes and create designs from them. And, by the time she was three, she was telling her dad ways to make the games even better!

"I need a rhombus for the wings!" Treeka said, as she set out to create a butterfly using her shapes on the computer.

Treeka wasn't just a fan of computer games. She loved all types of games: brain games, board games, strategy games, card games, puzzles—you name it.

The more she played, the more she began to notice that there were tricks for winning some games and solving puzzles. In fact, the harder it was to figure out how to win a game or solve a puzzle, the more fun it was.

"Oh, this one is extra tricky," she grinned as she rotated a puzzle cube in her hands. "No prob."

Sometimes Treeka resorted to "creative" puzzle solutions. Like the time she "solved" her Rubik's Cube by prying it apart with a screwdriver and reassembling it with the colors in their proper position.

ONE THING TREEKA *DIDN'T* LIKE WAS MORNINGS. SHE NEVER seemed to have enough time to get ready for school.

"I noticed that you get distracted picking out a shirt to wear," her mother told her.

"That's true. It's so hard to choose," Treeka explained as she pointed into her closet, which was filled with dozens of black t-shirts.

"You should create an algorithm to help you decide what to wear each morning," her mother suggested.

"What's an algorithm?" Treeka asked.

"An algorithm is a set of instructions you follow in order to solve a problem or do something—like deciding on what to wear for school," her mother explained.

Treeka eagerly accepted the challenge. That afternoon, she wrote her first algorithm. And from that day on, she never had a problem choosing a shirt to wear to school.

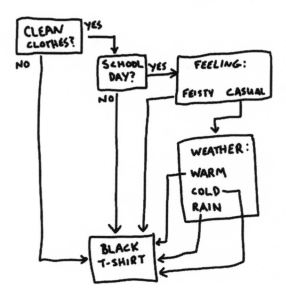

As Treeka grew older, she learned that she could create algorithms for many different things and use computer programs to run them. This is called *programming*.

She began to apply her new skills—programming computers to run her algorithms—to do EVERYTHING.

She wrote a program to solve puzzles faster.

She wrote a program to make up funny knock-knock jokes.

She wrote a program to make Blue Bear say, "Good idea, Treek," no matter what she said.

She even wrote a program to automatically order pizza when her parents had to work late.

"Mom has had a rough week, so I just added extra pepperoni to the pizza ordering algorithm," Treeka told Blue Bear.

"Good idea, Treek," Blue Bear replied.

"Why, thank you, Mr. Blue Bear," Treeka chuckled.

The only thing that intrigued Treeka more than writing programs was learning how to use secret codes. She loved making secret codes almost as much as she loved cracking them.

One of Treeka's happiest moments was when she wrote a program to make codes for sharing secret notes with her friend, Lilly, on the bus ride home from school.

One evening over dinner, Treeka's parents announced that her mother got a new job in a different state.

"We're moving to a new house—with a big yard that backs right up to a nature preserve," her mother explained to Treeka and her little brother, Stevie. "You'll have a huge forest as your back yard!" she added.

"And now that we'll have a bigger yard, we can finally get that drone you've been wanting," her father promised.

"What's a drone?" Stevie asked.

"It's a flying robot," Treeka said. "I'll teach you how to fly it," she promised.

Treeka was nervous about moving at first, but she was thrilled about learning how to fly the drone.

She started imagining all of the things she could program it to do.

THE DRONE ARRIVED A FEW DAYS BEFORE THE BIG MOVE. Treeka was absolutely thrilled!

She named it "Drone" because, well, it's a drone.

While the rest of her family helped the movers load the truck, Treeka practiced some cool stunts with Drone.

She swooped Drone up, down, left, right. She even flew it upside down!

Treeka was engrossed in Drone's acrobatics when, suddenly, Stevie's prized autographed soccer ball fell out of one of the moving boxes and started rolling down the street.

"My soccer ball!" cried Stevie.

Treeka looked over just in time to see the soccer ball rolling down the street.

It rolled faster and faster, gathering speed as it headed downhill.

"Oh no," said one of the movers. "It's going too fast. We'll never catch it now!"

Poor little Stevie looked at Treeka, tears welling up in his eyes.

"Don't worry, little brother," said Treeka. "I got this!"

With a steely glint in her eyes and an expert flick of her thumbs, Treeka worked the remote controller, summoning Drone.

Drone appeared out of nowhere and whizzed by them like a screeching eagle.

In a flash, Drone flew down the street, ahead of the ball, and lowered itself right in front of the ball's path.

Drone extended its two robotic arms and caught the rolling ball.

Then, Treeka used the controller to gently pilot Drone as it carried the ball back to where they were standing.

"My ball!" Stevie shrieked, delighted to have his ball back, safe and sound.

Treeka's mother came running out of the house. "What happened?!" she asked frantically.

"My ball ran away and Treeka saved it!" said Stevie. "Treek, you're my hero!"

"Thanks, little brother," Treeka said. "But I'm not the hero. Drone is the hero," she grinned.

Later that night, Treeka crawled into her sleeping bag in her mostly empty bedroom.

Her mind was too busy to sleep. This was nothing new, of course. But tonight, something was different.

She looked around her room. Most of her things were packed up and loaded into the moving truck, ready for the big moving day tomorrow. Only Blue Bear, her laptop, and Drone remained.

"They're too important to put in a moving truck," she had explained to her parents.

She thought about having a new room, in a new house, in a new neighborhood.

She wondered about the woods—so mysterious! She wondered about the new friends she would make.

Mostly, she thought about Drone. Today's "emergency" had just been about saving a soccer ball. But what if it had been a real emergency?

"I need a way to summon Drone, no matter where I am," said Treeka.

She looked at her clock. "In about six hours, we're moving to a new state."

"No problem. I can sleep in the car," she reassured herself.

Treeka climbed out of her sleeping bag, turned on her laptop computer, and started writing what would soon turn out to be the most important program she had ever written in her life.

3

EVELYN ENGINEER

*E*ngineers are the people who design and build the things that make our world easier to live in. They've invented almost everything you see around you, from small things like nail clippers, toasters, and phones, to big things, like cars, buildings, and bridges. Engineers even build rocket ships!

There have been engineering masterminds for thousands of years, of course.

Many said that Evelyn would grow up to be one of the best engineers *ever*. Even as a baby, she was always eager to learn how things worked.

She took everything apart. *Everything!*

On her second birthday, Evelyn received a Jack-in-the-box from her grandma. It startled her poor dog, Beulah, but Evelyn was intrigued.

She had so many questions!

How many turns before Jack pops out?

What causes Jack to pop out of the box?

What happens if I turn the crank in the opposite direction?

Where does the music come from?

There was one way to get answers about her Jack-in-the-box...

She took it apart.

Inside the box, Evelyn found a puppet on a spring and a music box that released a latch when she cranked it exactly eighteen times.

"What else could I build with these parts?" Evelyn wondered.

And one hour and twenty-four minutes later, the "Treat Machine 2000" was invented.

AS EVELYN GREW, HER ENGINEERING FEATS BECAME MORE AND
more ambitious.

It seemed that there wasn't a problem that couldn't be solved
with a few parts from around the house and some creativity.

There was the noodle detangler...

The cat backscratcher...

The self-sharpening pencil...

The anti-theft candy wrappers...

And, her very favorite invention so far, the Ketchup Koater Version 2.0. (Don't ask about version 1.0.)

By the time she was ten, Evelyn had her own workshop.

Her parents were always eager to hear about her latest project. Sometimes she even built her own assistants.

She had so many ideas she wanted to test that she created a few robot"friends" to help her with less exciting projects (like chores).

ONE MORNING, EVELYN WAS AWAKENED BY HER DOG, BEULAH, who was whining outside her bedroom window. "It's too early, Beulah! Please play by yourself a bit longer," she begged.

Beulah became more and more distressed, so Evelyn crawled out of bed and went outside to see what was the matter.

"Do you need a toy?" Evelyn asked Beulah as she reached into the dog's toy box.

But the toy box was empty!

"That's odd," Evelyn murmured to herself. "We just bought new dog toys yesterday. Where are all of your toys, Beulah?"

Beulah just whimpered in reply.

Evelyn searched all over the backyard for Beulah's toys, but there were no signs of them.

"I guess we'll have to buy some more," she sighed, heading back into the house.

That night, Evelyn loaded up Beulah's toy box with plenty of new toys. "These should keep you happy for awhile," she said confidently.

The very next morning, Beulah was at her window again, whining for her attention. Evelyn went outside and, sure enough... Beulah's toy box was completely empty again.

She scoured the entire yard.

Again, there were no toys anywhere! However, this time, she spotted something new...

Tiny footprints!

Yes, tiny footprints.

Right there, in the dirt, next to the toy box.

Now she knew what the problem was. Someone... or some*thing*... was stealing Beulah's toys!

"I don't know who is stealing your toys, Beulah, but I do know how to find out," Evelyn assured her.

Evelyn had developed quite a reputation for building traps from which even the most clever trespassing critters could never escape.

Like many traps, Evelyn's traps were designed to be triggered by the actions of the offending critter—in this case, the critter who was stealing brand new toys that belong to her family dog.

With some simple tools, a few scraps of lumber, and the right bait, Evelyn could trap just about anything.

She always released her captive back into the wild, just far enough away to correct their trespassing habits.

Evelyn was eager to use her trapping skills, so she hurried into her workshop, where she sketched, and measured, and drilled, and hammered away until lunchtime.

Later that night, Evelyn presented her newest project to Beulah.

"Behold, my newest invention—The Trespasser Trapper 3000," she beamed.

Beulah just sat there, looking puzzled.

"When the thief goes into the box," Evelyn explained, "this motion detector will trigger this solenoid, which will release that latch, which will drop this lid down, and BAM! The trespasser is trapped!"

Beulah wagged her tail with excitement.

Evelyn set up the Trespasser Trapper 3000 in the back yard and ducked inside the house to wait for her plan to unfold.

A LITTLE AFTER NINE O'CLOCK, WHEN IT WAS COMPLETELY DARK

outside, there was a loud "CLUNK!" sound and the backyard suddenly lit up.

"Let's go!" Evelyn screeched in delight, as she grabbed her flashlight and ran out to the backyard to catch a glimpse of the culprit.

There, in the spotlight, sat a small raccoon, looking very guilty, clutching Beulah's brand-new chew toy in its tiny little hands.

"It's time for you to find a new place to play," Evelyn scolded. She went back inside to tell her parents so they could relocate the raccoon and release it into the woods.

THE NEXT MORNING, BEULAH PLAYED HAPPILY IN THE YARD with her toys while Evelyn slept in, much later than usual.

"Look at the time!" exclaimed Evelyn when she finally roused. "It's time to get going. Today is a big day!" she reminded herself.

Her friend Mattie was having a slumber party that night. Evelyn had promised to introduce her latest, greatest invention to her friends at the party.

It was something even cooler than the Trespasser Trapper 3000. Something top secret that she had been working on for months.

4

ARIANA ARTIST

*A*riana entered the world during a warm but rainy summer day.

"We needed some rain. You're our little good luck charm," her mother whispered into her tiny ear.

Ariana gazed out of the hospital window to admire the big, bright rainbow that welcomed her.

From the moment her eyes opened each morning until they slowly closed at night, baby Ariana eagerly observed the world around her. She was delighted to discover beautiful patterns in nearly everything she saw.

There were patterns in clouds.

There were patterns in cat fur.

There were patterns in kiwi slices.

There were patterns in rain drops.

There were even patterns in the fern that her grandma brought back from her trip to Costa Rica.

BABY ARIANA SOON LEARNED THAT SHE COULD MAKE HER OWN patterns—and actually, all types of designs—using just about anything she could get her hands on.

To Ariana, the sky was the limit. She created masterpieces everywhere and out of everything.

Feathers made great paint brushes.

Beans became mosaics.

Leaves morphed into wings.

She even learned how to make curvy lines out of straight lines and fantastic sculptures out of kitchen garbage!

As Ariana grew older, her palette grew larger. Oil, acrylic, and watercolor paint in every color you can imagine flowed softly, yet purposefully, from her fingers.

Her parents let her paint anything she wanted on one special wall of the house, which they called "Ariana's wall." When the wall was all filled up with paint, she would paint new

parts over the old parts, so her wall and art would continu-
ously evolve.

She loved that her wall was always changing, and never
finished, just like her.

Whenever Ariana was about to paint over a section of her
wall, she always stopped to take a picture first so she could
keep a record of the wall as it changed over time.

BY THE TIME SHE WAS 10, ARIANA HAD BECOME QUITE SKILLED
at photography. Using a camera, Ariana created art by
"painting with light" and freezing time in a photograph.

She took her camera everywhere, and she loved how her
collection of photos all combined to tell the story about
her life.

She learned a computer program called Photoshop, which
let her do things with her photographs that seemed almost
like magic!

She could stretch them, squeeze them, rotate them, lighten
them, darken them, erase parts, copy parts, and even
combine her photos together to create an entirely new
picture. In time, Ariana learned to create any image in the
computer that she could imagine in her mind.

ARIANA LOVED PAINTING AND PHOTOGRAPHY, BUT HER FAVORITE thing of all was molding things in clay. Clay allowed her to make *real objects* that she could hold in her hands and see from every angle. The objects she created were sometimes useful, sometimes beautiful, and sometimes both beautiful and useful at the same time.

Sometimes her clay objects were goofy-looking or lopsided. It didn't matter because Ariana could always just squish the clay back into a ball and start all over until she got exactly what she wanted.

On occasion, she made a mistake and created something wonderful that she hadn't planned at all. She called these creations her "happy accidents." Ariana's happy accidents were some of the best things she ever created.

And sometimes Ariana used her artistic skills to solve a problem or make an idea come to life.

ONE AFTERNOON, A LARGE BOX ARRIVED AT ARIANA'S HOUSE. "Open it up," said Ariana's parents, glancing slyly at one another.

Ariana slowly opened the box, revealing something she had wanted for as long as she could remember...

"A 3D PRINTER!!" Ariana rejoiced.

A 3D printer is a machine that lets you "print" real objects from a computer.

Ariana quickly learned how to use a special computer program to stretch, squeeze, and make all kinds of changes to objects, just like she had done to her pictures in Photoshop.

But now, she could print out the objects she created and *hold them in her hands!*

And, better still, she could design the objects that she created *to do something.*

Ariana's world would never be the same.

One Saturday afternoon, Ariana's friend Evelyn dropped by to ask for help. Evelyn had set up a lemonade and green tea stand at 8:00 AM, and she hadn't had a single customer yet.

"There's a soccer tournament at the park, so I set up my stand on the corner," said Evelyn. "According to my estimates, I should have made $18.50 by now."

Ariana was surprised as well. "That should be a really good location. Let's take a look and maybe we can figure what's wrong."

She grabbed a notepad and pencil and headed out the door with Evelyn.

Ariana stood by the entrance of the park and asked the people who passed through it a few questions.

"Do you like lemonade? How about green tea? Did you bring your own drinks to the game? Would you pay 25 cents for one? Why didn't you stop by the lemonade and green tea stand on the corner when you walked by?"

Ariana learned that most of the people liked lemonade. Some people liked green tea. Only half of the people brought their own drinks. And, almost everyone thought the price was very reasonable.

But, wait—aha!—none of them had realized the lemonade and green tea stand even existed!

It turns out the stand's sign was not readable from the

parking lot because the letters were too small and the sign's colors blended into the background.

"The problem isn't the drinks or the price," Ariana explained to Evelyn. *"It's the sign. People can't see it from the parking lot."*

Ariana knew just what to do. She rushed home to make a new sign. She returned to the park in about an hour with the most beautiful sign Evelyn could have imagined.

"Wow, that sign is amazing! It'll get a lot of attention for sure!" Evelyn beamed.

It was a hot day and people were thirsty. Evelyn was right. Within minutes, a line had formed around the corner.

ARIANA OFFERED TO STAY AND HELP EVELYN WITH ALL OF HER new customers.

They worked non-stop for hours, but the time flew by. Before they knew it, the final game was over. The crowds dispersed, and Evelyn poured one final drink, bidding her last customer a cheerful, "Thanks and have a great day!"

"Wow!" said Evelyn as she started counting the money in the cash box. "We made almost $60! And I do mean *we*," she said, as she handed half of the money to Ariana.

"Thanks so much for your help. I never could have done it

without your help and your amazing sign-making superpowers!"

"Oh, thank you, but that's not necessary," said Ariana. "You bought all of the supplies. I enjoyed just hanging out with you and talking to all these nice people."

"Besides," she added, "I've got my Web design business, and I know you planned this event to earn money for your project."

"What's the project again?" Ariana probed.

"I'm saving to buy an electric motor for my latest invention, which I plan to unveil at Mattie's slumber party next weekend," said Evelyn. "If tomorrow's sales are anything like today, I'll have more than enough!"

"No doubt!" Ariana said.

Ariana paused to think for a moment.

"You know," she said, "several times today, I noticed some people stopped to buy a drink, but they left because the line was too long."

"Yes," said Evelyn. "I saw that, too. I'm sure we could sell more if we increased our throughput, but I just don't think I can pour any faster.

Ariana paused again to think about the problem. She closed her eyes, taking long, deep breaths.

"Oooh," Evelyn observed quietly. "I love it when you go to your creative place! Never know what we're gonna find in there."

Evelyn watched patiently as Ariana, eyes still shut, whispered calmly to herself, "almost there... taking shape... al... most... there..."

"I've got it!" Ariana declared suddenly, snapping her fingers, eyes opening wide as she burst out in a giant grin.

"Got what?" asked Evelyn.

"*Peace!*" exclaimed Ariana.

"Piece? Piece of what?" asked Evelyn.

"Not piece. PEACE!" said Ariana. "Your shirt!"

Evelyn looked down at the peace symbol on her t-shirt.

"Peace?" asked Evelyn. She was confused.

"Drop by my house tonight at eight o'clock," said Ariana.

"I have an idea—oh, and I'm going to need to borrow this," Ariana said as she snatched the pitcher out of Evelyn's hands and hurried home.

Evelyn was intrigued.

ARIANA RACED HOME. SHE SPENT THE NEXT HOUR TAKING measurements of the pitcher and clicking away at her computer.

"Aaaaand ... print!" she said, once she was satisfied with her work.

Suddenly, Ariana's 3D printer sprang to life. Lights started flashing and metal parts inside the printer began to zig and zag, making "zzztzzztzzzt" noises with each speedy motion.

The printer started building an object by adding thousands of thin layers of soft plastic, one on top of the other. As each layer hardened, a new one followed.

Soon, an object started to take shape.

Ariana left to eat dinner while her 3D printer continued humming away.

AT PRECISELY EIGHT O'CLOCK AND ZERO SECONDS, THE
doorbell rang. (Evelyn was never late.)

"You're just in time!" said Ariana, as she opened the door.
"I'm just about to do my first test!" she explained as the two
girls walked into her studio.

There, on a table in the middle of the room, sat something
covered under a cloth, next to three empty cups.

"Ta-dah!" Ariana announced as she pulled away the cloth,
revealing her 3D-printed creation.

"Peace!" shouted Evelyn. "I get it now. You made a... spout...
shaped like the peace symbol on my t-shirt."

"Exactly!" cried Ariana. "Check this out!" grinned Ariana, as
she used her new creation to fill three cups of water at once
without spilling a drop.

"This should increase our... through... what did you call it?"

"Throughput," said Evelyn.

"It should increase our throughput by a factor of three!" exclaimed Ariana.

"I love it!" Evelyn squealed.

"Have you... named it yet?" Evelyn ventured, cautiously.

"Why, no I hav..." Ariana began.

"MULTI-POUR 5700!" shouted Evelyn, beaming.

"Sure, why not," said Ariana. "Multi-Pour 5700 it is!"

And with the click of the mouse, Ariana printed a second Multi-Pour 5700 so that they would have one for lemonade and one for green tea.

The next day, using her two Multi-Pour 5700's, Evelyn and Ariana served customers three at a time and they made three times more money than the day before!

"Look at us, a couple of entrepreneurs," Evelyn smiled. "Looks like I'll be able to afford a top-of-the line electric motor now!"

"Excellent!" said Ariana. "What's the motor for?" asked Ariana, nonchalantly.

"Ha! Nice try... it's still a surprise," Evelyn grinned. "You're just going to have to wait for Mattie's slumber party to find out."

5

MATTIE MATHEMATICIAN

Mattie was born with a love for solving problems. In fact, at KinderGym, she was the fastest shape sorter her teachers had ever seen.

Things got even more exciting for Mattie when she started learning how to count.

Mattie liked to count all of her favorite things.

First, she learned to count one item at a time. But the number 3 was her favorite number. She liked to count out 3's of things everywhere she went. She grouped *everything* by 3.

Her parents would smile and say, "There's our little Mattie, the Mathematician."

In time, her love of numbers helped her see beautiful patterns all around her.

Numbers let her think about the world in a whole new way and solve all kinds of problems.

She loved to sort, stack, make shapes, count, and build puzzles. More than anything, though, Mattie loved to eat cream cheese and carrot sandwiches (which are more delicious than you might think).

When Mattie's mother made her sandwiches, she cut them into four long rectangles.

When her father made them, he cut them into four triangles.

Mattie knew the shape of her sandwich didn't matter. No matter how they were cut, they were exactly the same size. And they were delicious!

As Mattie grew, her fascination with numbers grew,

too. Instead of counting each of her favorite things, she learned to estimate them instead.

"Sometimes," Mattie said, "being close is good enough."

Mattie even realized that, by estimating, she could sort of predict the *future!*

Hmmm... at my current rate of one cream cheese and carrot sandwich per day, thought Mattie, *I will eat 34,675 sandwiches by the time I'm 100 years old!*

To Mattie, playing with numbers was like playing with an imaginary version of the world. She felt that almost any question could be answered using math.

"Our tent is 14 feet long and 9 feet wide," said Mattie's father. "How many sleeping bags can you fit into it for your slumber party?" he asked her.

"Easy peasy!" said Mattie. She quickly noticed that there were a few different ways to solve the problem.

"Many problems have more than one solution," said Mattie's father with a smile.

"Always be on the lookout for a better way."

THE NEXT DAY, AS MATTIE AND HER DOG, FIBONACCI, WERE IN the garden counting rosebuds, she spotted something unusual in front of the house next door.

"Look Fibbo! A moving truck!" said Mattie. Fibbo's ears perked up.

"I think we have new neighbors," she told Fibbo. The two of them went to get a closer look.

The moving truck was towing a greenish-blue minivan with a Nebraska license plate.

"Wow, Nebraska!" Mattie said. "That's pretty far away."

She pulled up a map on her watch and did a quick calculation. "Nebraska is about 1,600 miles away. I estimate that it took that truck about twenty-five hours to get here."

She watched curiously for hours as the movers emptied the truck. She saw a bike, a kiddie pool, some toys, and other kid-sized stuff.

"Kids!" thought Mattie, looking at the toys. However, there were no kids to be seen anywhere.

She wondered what kids from Nebraska look like. And were they boys or girls?

Just then, she spotted two children. Unfortunately, it was getting too dark to see them clearly.

"How many ways could there be a mix of boys and girls?" Mattie wondered.

She pointed her finger and drew a quick sketch in the air. When she was away from her whiteboard, drawing an imaginary picture helped her visualize, or "see" the problem in her mind.

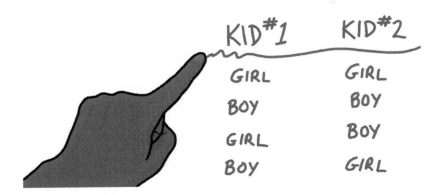

Mattie was determined to find out who was moving into the house next door.

Even more important, she wanted to know if any of them loved math.

THE NEXT MORNING, AS SOON AS SHE WOKE UP, SHE BOUNCED out of bed, brushed her teeth, and headed over to introduce herself.

Mattie knocked on the neighbor's door. A young girl answered. "Hello, I'm Mattie, your neighbor to the left," Mattie chirped.

"Hi! I'm Treeka, short for Teresa," the girl answered.

Mattie asked, "How many of you live here?"

"Well, we had six before we left, and now we're down to five. Sadly, a member of our family has escaped," Treeka sighed.

"Escaped?!" gasped Mattie.

"I moved here with my two parents," said Treeka, "and my little brother, Stevie, short for Esteban."

"Plus my cat," Treeka continued. "And Fred," she sighed.

Treeka closed her eyes, shaking her head. "Stevie took Fred out exploring last night without a flashlight, and Fred escaped! We searched for hours but couldn't find him anywhere. Although I'm pretty sure I heard him croaking."

"Oh, no!" gasped Mattie. "Croaking?"

"Oh, I should have mentioned," Treeka chuckled. "Fred is a tree frog."

"A tree frog? Neat!" said Mattie. She started tapping away on her watch. "It says here that tree frogs will seek out water to stay moist."

Mattie quickly scanned the yard. She spotted the kiddie pool, and announced, "I have an idea!"

Mattie pulled a garden hose over and began to fill the kiddie pool.

"Tree frogs aren't very good swimmers," Treeka warned her.

"No problem. We'll just fill the pool enough to cover most of his body," Mattie suggested. "Two inches should do the trick."

"Right-o," Treeka agreed.

Mattie glanced at her watch. "A half inch in 15 seconds," she mumbled to herself.

"At this rate, the water should be two inches deep in about 45 more seconds."

Exactly 45 seconds later, the water was exactly two inches deep. Mattie turned off the water.

"Now, we wait," said Mattie.

Minutes later, a frog appeared out of the tall grass and plopped right into the pool with a splash.

"Fred!" Treeka shrieked in delight.

"Hi, Fred!" said Mattie. "Nice to meet you!"

"And you, too, Treeka," Mattie continued. "Welcome to the neighborhood!"

"Thank you!" said Treeka. "I love it here!"

"I'm having a slumber party on Saturday," said Mattie.

"Would you like to come? I can't wait to introduce you to the kids from the neighborhood!"

"I'd love to!" Treeka beamed.

Mattie was thrilled to have a brand new friend move in right next door. She imagined that they would have amazing adventures together.

Little did Mattie know that she and her friends were about to embark on the adventure of a lifetime.

PART II

STEAMTEAM 5

6

SLUMBER PARTY

*I*t was late Saturday afternoon, and Mattie was very excited. She had become a local legend for her amazing backyard campout summer slumber parties. This was to be her first party of the summer!

She sat on her bed, playing Bach's Endless Canon on her electric guitar for her dog, Fibonacci.

Mattie paused her playing. "It's mathematically the most beautiful piece of music ever written," she explained. "Bach was probably an alien."

Fibbo wagged his tail.

Suddenly, Mattie's watch beeped with a text alert.

"Ready 2 set up tent?" the text read. It was from Sandia.

Mattie fired back a reply:

Moments later, Sandia was standing at Mattie's front door, loaded up with her sleeping bag and duffel bag in one arm and her very large telescope in the other.

"Let me help you with that," Mattie's father offered as he took the telescope from her.

"So, have you figured out where to set up the tent yet?" Mattie's father asked them.

Sandia had her answer ready. "We should face the opening of the tent away from the house so we can watch the sky from inside the tent."

"There'll be a new moon tonight," she added.

"What's a new moon?" asked Mattie.

"It's when the moon passes between the sun and earth, and it basically becomes invisible to us. The sky will be extra dark, so it's easier to see stars and look at deep-sky objects like galaxies, star clusters, and nebulae."

"Awesome!" said Mattie. "I can't wait!"

"It gets even better!" said Sandia. "Last night, I met our new neighbor, Treeka, and she had a great idea about how to make my telescope even more fun. I don't want to spoil the surprise, so I'll show everyone later, when it's dark enough."

"Oh, I've met Treeka, too!" said Mattie. "I helped her find her escaped frog."

Then, as if on cue, the doorbell rang.

"Hi, Treeka, come on in!" said Mattie, as she opened the door.

Ariana arrived next.

"Nice to meet you! I'm Treeka, short for Teresa," said Treeka.

"Hi! I'm Ariana," Ariana smiled, as she shook Treeka's hand. "I heard you were coming. Welcome to the neighborhood!"

"Did everyone bring a surprise?" asked Mattie.

"Yes!" said Treeka and Sandia.

"I brought my surprise, too," said Ariana.

"But mostly, I can't wait to see what Evelyn brings! She's been building something big for months. I wonder where she is. It's six o'clock exactly and Evelyn is never la..."

Just then, the girls heard a buzzing sound and were shocked to see Evelyn, wearing a helmet, elbow pads, and kneepads, zooming toward them on an electric skateboard.

Evelyn veered off the road onto a small dirt hill, jumping over a shrub and landing perfectly.

"Hi everybody!" shouted Evelyn, as she sailed up the driveway and screeched to a stop.

"Wow! That sure is a sweet ride! I'm Treeka, short for Teresa. I just moved into the house between Sandia and Mattie."

"Thanks! I'm Evelyn. This is my surprise... it's my latest invention, a motorized, off-road skateboard. I call her EV-1."

"Short for Electric Vehicle-1?" asked Treeka.

"Whoa," said Evelyn. "I never thought of that. Well, it *was* short for *Evelyn-1*. But I guess it can be both!"

"Okay, that was *definitely* worth waiting to see," said Ariana as she checked out Evelyn's new ride.

"A motor? Wow. How fast does it go?" Sandia inquired.

"We shall see," grinned Evelyn.

"Impressive," added Treeka.

"Now that introductions are over, let's go to my project room, and I'll show all of you *my* surprise," said Mattie.

"Platonic solids!" declared Mattie, throwing her hands into the air as she presented her project.

Sandia blinked, not sure she understood. "You... made these shapes out of popsicle sticks and glue?"

"Oh n-n-n-n-no... not just any shapes," said Mattie, wagging her finger.

"Special shapes!" she added.

"Tetrahedrons, cubes, octahedrons, icosahedrons... but yes, Popsicle sticks and glue. I clamp them with clothespins while the glue dries," she said, cheerfully.

She moved aside to share her favorite. "This one is my pride-and-joy," Mattie continued.

"It's a *dodecahedron*—a twelve-sided object made of pentagons. It was discovered by the Pythagoreans in ancient Greece, and they kept it a secret. They thought it was magical!"

"I could make models of molecules with these sticks!" said Sandia.

"I could make a castle!" exclaimed Ariana.

"Or medieval siege weapons!" exclaimed Evelyn.

"Or puzzle boxes!" exclaimed Treeka.

THEY ALL WENT INTO THE BACKYARD AND UNPACKED THEIR stuff inside of the tent.

Ariana was next to share her surprise. She took a small leather pouch out of her backpack and opened it, removing five friendship bracelets.

"I made everybody a bracelet!" said Ariana. "Heh, and well, ok, one for myself, too... so we would all match."

"Each bracelet has all our initials... S – T – E – A – M... for Sandia, Treeka, Evelyn, me, and Mattie."

"Look!" cried Sandia. "It spells STEAM!"

"I like steam," said Evelyn. "Thank you, Ariana. That was very sweet of you."

Everybody agreed and thanked Ariana for her thoughtful surprise gift.

TREEKA'S SURPRISE CAME NEXT. SHE PULLED A STACK OF DISC-shaped objects from her backpack and started passing them out to all the girls.

"Cipher wheels!" said Treeka.

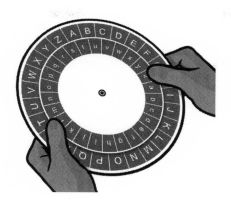

"With these, we can send secret messages to each other. Nobody else can read them unless they have one of these wheels!"

"Cryptography! Cool!" Mattie chimed in.

"Yes," Treeka responded. Cryptography is the science of using secret codes.

Sandia pulled out her notebook and tore out five pieces of paper.

"Here!" she said as she passed out the paper. "Let's give it a try!"

"It works like this..." Treeka began. "First you choose two letters—one from each wheel—to be the secret letters. For example, I'll choose 'Z' as the secret letter for the outer wheel and 'S' for the letter for the inner wheel. Then, you line up the secret letters like this," she demonstrated as she rotated the wheel.

"Then," she continued. "You write your secret message by using the letters on the outer wheel to replace the ones on the inner wheel."

"So, I'll write a 'Z' in place of an 'S," and 'A' instead of a 'T,' and so on," she explained as she wrote the letters on her paper.

"The person who receives the message uses the same configuration on the wheel to translate it," she added.

"Ta-da!"

They all squealed in delight and immediately started using their cipher wheels to write messages to each other.

As the sun went down, they ate pizza and laughed, played, sang songs, danced, and told jokes and stories.

Sandia was one of the best storytellers of all time. She told a spooky mystery that caught everyone by surprise at the end.

They all had a blast.

"It's time for my surprise now," said Sandia, looking out at the sky, which was now very dark.

She put on her white lab coat, which she always liked to wear while doing science.

"The other night, Treeka showed me how to add a camera to my telescope so we could take pictures of stars!" Sandia announced, as she pointed outside the tent at the telescope.

Mattie gasped in delight. Ariana and Evelyn cheered enthusiastically. Sandia pointed the telescope at Jupiter. Each of the girls took a turn looking at the bright planet.

"Is there something wrong with your telescope, Sandia?" asked Ariana when it was her turn.

"I'm seeing four little reflections or something, right next to Jupiter, in a line."

Sandia's eyes flashed as she lit up with a smile. "There's nothing wrong with the telescope, Ariana."

"Those are moons! Jupiter's four biggest moons, the Galilean moons—Io, Europa, Ganymede, and Callisto!"

Jupiter & Galilean Moons

Ariana looked again and gasped out loud. "They're so beautiful... they look like... diamonds! I'm going to paint this!" she said.

"I'll snap a picture for you, Ariana," said Treeka. "For you to use as a reference when you paint it."

"Oh, that would be wonderful! Thank you!" said Ariana.

As the night wore on, one by one, the girls drifted off to sleep. Even Mattie's dog, Fibbo, was snoring away. The last to fall asleep was night owl Treeka.

"I love my new friends," she thought, as her dreams finally carried her away.

Soon, the only sound you could hear was the wind blowing through the trees and an occasional hoot of a Great Grey Owl.

In the wee hours of the morning, their slumber was suddenly—and quite loudly—interrupted.

Mattie heard a crashing sound and sat up quickly, scanning the tent for Fibonacci.

"Fibbo!" she called out in a loud whisper, trying not to wake the others. But the dog was not inside the tent.

Somewhere out in the yard, Fibbo began barking loudly, which woke up the other girls.

"What's wrong?" Sandia asked, rubbing her eyes.

"Not sure. I'll go check," Mattie said.

"Let's all go. Flashlights, everybody," said Sandia, snapping into action.

All five girls grabbed their gear and headed out into the darkness.

7

INTO THE DARKNESS

The girls continued to call out for Fibbo. Mattie heard him growling at something in the darkness.

"Fibbo, come here!" she demanded. But he did not follow her command.

"It's so dark without the moon," Ariana noted.

"This is unlike him," Mattie told the others. "There must be something out there in the woods."

"Creeeeepy!" said Ariana.

"Coooool!" said Treeka.

"Shine your lights in the bushes," Evelyn suggested. "These

woods are full of all kinds of critters that mostly come out at night. Mostly."

In the beam of a flashlight there appeared two little red glowing eyes."

"Aaaaaah!" screamed all of the girls, except Evelyn, who just nodded with a smile.

"Mm-hmm, I thought so," said Evelyn. "Looks like somebody found her way back to this neighborhood."

"Wh-what is it?" asked Ariana, almost afraid to ask.

"I'm guessing it's a raccoon," said Evelyn. "Maybe the same one I caught stealing Beulah's toys."

"Hello, Cartwright," Mattie smirked.

"Cartwright?" asked Sandia.

"Yeah, she creates so much chaos that we named her after Mary Cartwright, one of the first mathematicians to study what would later become known as chaos theory."

Suddenly, the creature jumped out of the bushes and bolted through a broken gate. The girls all saw its big, bushy, striped tail. Yes, indeed! It was a raccoon.

Fibbo started barking and chased the raccoon, right through the broken gate and into the darkness of the forest.

"Fibbo!" Mattie called out as she pulled the gate wide open

and chased after both of them. She began whistling for her dog, but he ignored that, too.

Ariana, Evelyn, Treeka, and Sandia followed her.

Evelyn hopped onto her skateboard. "Follow me!" she called out to the others as she raced down the trail toward the sound of Fibbo's bark.

Despite going as fast as they could, they couldn't catch up to Fibbo or his furry little bandit-masked nemesis.

Soon, Fibbo's bark faded into the distance.

The girls had to stop to take a break. They were exhausted from running as fast as they could through the trees—well, except for Evelyn, who skidded to a stop on her skateboard to join them.

They scanned the trees with their flashlights. Fibbo was nowhere to be seen, and they could no longer hear his barks.

Just when they were about to lose all hope, Sandia's science instincts kicked in.

"*Always be observing...*" she whispered to herself.

She pulled her trusty magnifying glass out of her lab coat pocket. She pointed her flashlight and the magnifying glass at the ground as she walked back and forth, in a careful pattern, so as not to miss any spot of ground near the path. The others watched her, fascinated.

"Tracks!" Sandia exclaimed.

The girls all gathered around her, excited. "See these claws and two lobes at the bottom? That's canine – cats have retractable claws and three lobes – so we can rule out bobcats."

"It's too small for a wolf and the wrong toe placement for a fox. That leaves canis lupis familiaris… domesticated dog."

"Fibbo?'" inquired Mattie.

"Maybe," said Sandia. "The tracks look fresh. If our hypothesis is correct, we should also see…"

"Over here!" exclaimed Ariana.

"Look, tracks," she said, pointing her flashlight at the ground near the dog tracks.

"Good work!" said Sandia to Ariana. "Those are raccoon prints! Yes, I do believe we're on the *right track*... so to speak."

"But I'm afraid..." Sandia paused, looking into the darkness. "It's going to be slow-going tracking him in this darkness."

"The sun will be up in about an hour, and I'm afraid of how far he might go."

"If only we had a way to see in the dark," sighed Ariana.

Treeka gasped. "Of course!... Ariana, we DO have a way to see in the dark! And move much faster!"

Treeka pulled out her phone and tapped on the app she wrote the night before she moved—the one that she had named "Launch Drone."

8

DRONE TO THE RESCUE

Two miles away, something started happening in the darkness of Treeka's backyard.

Drone started to power up, red and green lights flashing, its four propellers starting to spin.

It was making a high-pitch buzzing sound like a thousand angry bees.

BZZZZZZ!

Drone's camera spun around, making a quick safety check. All clear. In an instant, it launched straight up into the sky and headed toward the GPS coordinates of Treeka's phone, using its built-in sensors to avoid colliding with trees.

Drone's two small robotic arms carried something beneath it.

Treeka looked at her phone.

"My drone will be here in two minutes." Treeka said.

"Your phone can summon... male reproductive bees?" Sandia asked.

"Heh, I wish," said Treeka. "No, Drone is my quadcopter. It's like a flying robot."

"You... have *a drone?*" asked Evelyn, mouth hanging open. "Girl, I'm in heaven!"

"I could use your help modding it!" said Treeka. "I'm good with software but I could really use your help designing custom parts. But we'd need a way to make them. If only I had a..."

"*3D printer!*" Ariana interrupted, finishing her sentence.

"I just got one! Oh, yeah, I'm trackin' with ya," said Ariana.

"Whoa, you have a 3D printer?" asked Treeka. "Game changing. Do you realize all the stuff we could..."

Just then, a faint buzzing sound could be heard from the southwest. It was getting louder.

"Drone!" Mattie shouted, pointing high above the treetops.

Treeka walked to a clearing and tapped a few instructions into her phone as Drone descended, landing gently nearby.

Drone set the object it had been carrying gently on the ground and whizzed back up into the sky.

"That's too cool..." murmured Ariana, snapping a photo of Drone as he ascended above the trees.

Treeka picked up the object and walked back to the group to show it to them.

"It's Drone's controller," she said.

"I can only summon him with my phone, and he can't do anything complicated on autopilot," said Treeka.

"With this controller, I can fly him almost anywhere, and we can see what he sees!"

"Can he help us find Fibbo?" asked Mattie. "You said something about seeing in the dark."

"Yes!" said Treeka. "I've equipped Drone with a thermal

imaging system I hacked together from an old point-n-shoot camera my dad was going to recycle."

The girls crowded around the video screen while Treeka navigated Drone.

"If these trees aren't too thick, Fibbo and his raccoon friend should stick out like a sore thumb on this display!" said Sandia.

"All objects warmer than absolute zero emit infrared radiation that can be detected by thermal imaging systems—which is basically a camera with a heat sensor," she explained.

"And, since animals are warmer than their surroundings when it's cool out, thermal cameras are perfect for searching for them at night," she continued.

"I recommend a grid search pattern along Fibbo's last known trajectory," said Mattie.

"That way," she pointed.

"This could take time," said Ariana.

"Especially if Fibbo kept running fast," said Sandia, "or if we have a lot of false positives—animals that aren't Fibbo—showing up on Drone's camera."

"I upgraded Drone's battery, but he can still only fly for about 40 minutes," Treeka cautioned.

Just then, a bright, white image appeared on the screen.

"*Is that him?*" Sandia asked.

Treeka zoomed in on the animal. A squirrel appeared on the display.

"Oh, it's just a squirrel," said Sandia.

It was the first of many false positives. The girls spent the next half hour huddled around the glowing screen as Treeka expertly piloted Drone back and forth, zooming in to inspect every white spot on the screen.

They found a lot of squirrels, nesting birds, a fox, and a family of raccoons. But no Fibbo.

The controller started to beep, and a low battery warning flashed.

"Only two minutes of battery left," Treeka said.

"Oh no, what will we do now?" asked Mattie. She was very worried about finding her dog.

At that moment, a new shape of an animal appeared on the screen, larger than the previous white figures.

"Zoom in!" Sandia exclaimed.

Treeka zoomed in.

"It's Fibbo!" Mattie rejoiced.

"Where is he?" Sandia asked.

"About 400 meters northeast of us," Treeka said, pointing into the forest. "Let's go!"

They all hurried in the direction of Fibbo and Drone.

Between the trees, to the east, the sky started to show a faint blue light over the horizon. It would soon be dawn.

Suddenly, an alarm sounded. A message appeared on Treeka's controller: "Battery low. Initiating soft landing and system shutdown."

Drone gently landed himself, and went to sleep.

The thermal image of Fibbo on Treeka's controller went black.

9

SIMPLE MACHINES

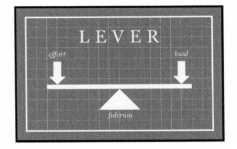

"Oh no! We'll never find Drone or Fibbo now," Sandia gasped.

"Don't worry," said Treeka. "Drone's main battery died, but we can still track him.

His GPS has a backup battery, for situations just like this."

They continued to follow the path shown on Treeka's drone controller.

At last, they came upon an old, narrow, long-forgotten road. It was so grown over with grass and shrubs that it was barely distinguishable from the forest.

"This must be an old logging road," noted Sandia. "Strange, I don't remember seeing it on any of my topo maps."

"Look, there's Drone!" shouted Evelyn, pointing at the downed quadcopter.

The girls ran over to it, nestled gently in the tall green grass. It was in perfect condition.

Sadly, Fibbo was nowhere to be seen.

The girls shined their flashlights through the dense trees and blackberry bushes and up and down the grown-over roadway.

"Fibbo!" called Mattie.

At first, they could hear only the wind blowing gently through the treetops. But then Ariana caught the faintest hint of a sound upon the breeze.

"What's that noise?" Ariana whispered.

They all stood very still and listened.

There it was again! They all heard it this time—it was a dog barking! Yet, it sounded strange, like a dog from another world.

"That's Fibbo's bark!" cried Mattie. "But he sounds... weird."

"Is that an echo I hear?" asked Evelyn, furrowing her eyebrow. "What would cause an echo way out here?"

Fibbo barked again. "That way!" said Sandia.

"No this way!" said Ariana.

"I thought it came from over there," said Treeka.

They were all confused. They did not see him anywhere.

"It sounds like he's... *everywhere!*" exclaimed Ariana.

"We're in a dell, along the side of a mountain," observed Sandia.

"Like where fairies and gnomes live?" asked Evelyn.

"The acoustics are making it hard to localize the sound," said Sandia. "Treeka, can you pull up the last thermal image that Drone shot of Fibbo?"

"Yes!" said Treeka. "I recorded the entire flight. Just a sec."

Treeka tapped a few instructions into her controller. "Got it!"

The girls gathered around and inspected the thermal image.

"What is that strange shape in the ground?" Ariana asked.

"Good question," Mattie replied. "Let's find out!"

Everyone spread out, flashlights in hand, to search for the object on the screen.

"Ouch!" Ariana cried out from a distance. The others ran over to her.

Ariana had tripped over something and fallen. She remained sitting on the ground, looking up at the rest of them.

"I think I found it," Ariana snickered as she shined her flashlight on a cement structure protruding from a pile of pine needles and leaves.

It was the same object they had seen on the drone's thermal image. She snapped a picture of it.

"Why would there be concrete way out here?" Sandia wondered out loud.

Sandia brushed away a few inches of leaves and soil, revealing concrete pavement beneath the dirt.

"Curious indeed!" said Sandia. "Not just blacktop, but concrete. I don't think this was just any old logging road."

"Ruff!" barked Fibbo.

It sounded like he was sitting right there with them, but his bark created a cavernous sounding echo.

"Look!" said Mattie. "Behind Ariana! There's an opening in the ground!"

The girls rushed over and shined their lights. It was, indeed, a hole in the ground.

Mattie brushed away some dirt, rocks, and brush, revealing a thick, rusted, iron grate.

"It looks like some kind of storm drain," said Sandia.

"Hmm," said Ariana, snapping a photo with a bright flash. "Isn't this kind of a strange place for a storm drain?" she asked. "I mean, way out here in the middle of the woods?"

"Very strange," said Evelyn. "You see drainage culverts under country roads all the time, but storm sewers are usually in towns."

The girls crouched down to look inside. They shined their flashlights into the drain and, suddenly – there he was!

Fibbo's eyes gazed up at them from the darkness far below. "Fibbo!" cried Mattie, her voice echoing. "I'm so happy to see you! How did you get down there, you little rascal?"

"He must have fallen into the opening above the grate," said Sandia. "There's no way he can come back out the same way. He's too far down to climb out."

"We'll have to lift the grate off," said Mattie.

Everyone tried to lift the grate, but it wouldn't budge.

"It's too heavy," said Sandia. "Should we go for help?"

"Nothing's too heavy," Evelyn winked. "All we need is a little mechanical advantage."

"What's mechanical advantage?" asked Treeka.

"It's when you use a machine to make you stronger," replied Evelyn.

"We're in the middle of the woods," said Mattie. "We don't have any machines with us."

"'*Give me a lever and a place to stand, and I will move the Earth!*'" said, Evelyn, quoting her hero, Archimedes. "Simple machines are everywhere!"

They were all intrigued.

"The type of simple machine we need to make is called a lever," she said. "It's like a seesaw."

"That's a really heavy grate. So, first, you need something long that's hard to break—like this!" she said as she lifted the end of a log from the ground nearby. She kicked the middle of the log, and it was solid. "Perfect!"

"Then you need a fulcrum," she continued. "It provides the support."

The farther away from the fulcrum we push down, the more the lever amplifies our weight," she explained.

"Here's our fulcrum," she said, rolling a short, stout log near the iron grate.

She lifted the long log on top of the fulcrum and inserted one end into a gap under the grate. Out of the corner of her eye, she spotted Ariana nodding as if she was predicting what would happen next.

Next, Evelyn walked over to the other end of the log where the girls were awaiting further instruction.

"On the count of three, everybody push down, and I'll jump onto the end. Our combined effort should easily overcome the load of the grate's weight," explained Evelyn.

"OK, get ready! One – two – three—and *PUSH!*" shouted Evelyn as she jumped onto the log in her skateboard-riding stance.

They all pushed down on the lever and the heavy iron storm drain popped out of its concrete enclosure like it weighed nothing at all.

It flung a few feet and landed on the ground with a heavy "CLUNK" sound.

"Ta-da!" said Evelyn, with a big smile, wiping her brow.

"Easy peasy!" said Mattie.

"That was fun!" added Sandia.

"I wish I had gotten a photo," sighed Ariana.

THE DRAIN WAS NOW WIDE OPEN. THE GIRLS PEERED DOWN into the darkness.

"Fibbo?" Mattie called down into the opening below.

Fibbo began barking.

"He's pretty far down, but there's a ladder," Mattie told the others. "I'm going in!" she said, quickly climbing down and disappearing from their view.

As soon as Mattie reached the bottom, Fibbo jumped into her arms and started licking her face.

"Fibbo! I'm so glad you're alright! What are you doing down here, you little irrational number?" she asked.

Fibbo whimpered softly. Mattie kissed him on the top of his head, and then retrieved her flashlight from her back pocket.

"Let's get some light on the subject," she said as she turned it on.

Mattie shined her flashlight all around. *Whoa. What is this place?* she wondered.

"Hey guys," she called up to the others.

"This place is weird... and kind of creepy. There's writing on the wall. It looks like a tunnel. I can't see the end."

The others looked nervously at one another, then nodded in agreement before, one by one, they cautiously climbed down the ladder into the unknown.

10

FORM FOLLOWS FUNCTION

*A*t the bottom of the ladder, the girls found themselves in a tube-shaped tunnel about ten feet in diameter.

"A dungeon crawl... sweet!" said Treeka.

Everyone turned on their flashlights. Even with the lights, they only saw complete darkness in each direction.

There was a sign on the wall that read "Evacuation Route" with arrows pointing to the right.

"Which way should we go?" asked Sandia.

"Let's follow the arrow. To the right," Ariana announced confidently. And so they went to the right.

By now, light from the rising sun made the entrance they had climbed down easy to find in the darkness of the tunnel.

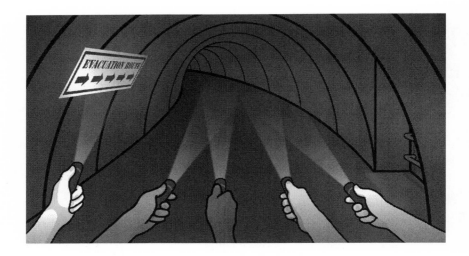

The tunnel was not straight; it curved gently to the left. They walked for about five minutes, after which they could go no farther. The tunnel was blocked by a pile of boulders and rubble.

"Looks like it caved in," said Sandia.

"Or was filled in," Evelyn suggested. "What is this place? If it's a storm sewer, who built it? And why?"

"And why is it curved?" Ariana added. "The road above us was straight, and I would expect a storm drain to follow the road."

"That's a good observation!" noted Sandia.

"Let's go back and try the other direction," said Ariana. And so they returned to the direction from which they came.

Walking in this direction, the tunnel curved to their right.

They soon passed the ladder where they had entered and they continued on past it. They continued walking for what seemed like a very long time. The tunnel always kept bending to the right.

"Are we walking in a giant circle?" Mattie asked.

"It sure feels like it," Treeka said.

Mattie started doing a quick calculation on her watch. "It's hard to say for sure without taking some measurements, but I estimate it would be a circle about—wow!—a mile or so in diameter!"

"Weird," said Evelyn. The others nodded, and they all kept walking.

"I wonder how far we've walked," said Ariana. "If we're walking in a circle, eventually we'll end up where we started. Or maybe to the other side of the pile of boulders, I guess."

"Why would somebody build a tunnel in the shape of a circle?" asked Evelyn. Nobody had any ideas.

The girls and Fibbo continued walking, quietly, in this mysterious place. It smelled old and musty. Suddenly, Ariana paused.

"Wait a minute!" said Ariana. "This isn't a circle! The curve is getting smaller."

"Are you sure?" asked Sandia. "How can you tell?"

"Look ahead," said Ariana.

"A few minutes ago, my flashlight's beam just disappeared in the darkness ahead of us. Now I can clearly see where it lands on the curved wall in front of us."

"The wall is closer... the curve is getting tighter!"

Mattie looked startled by this. She stopped and shined her flashlight ahead, then behind them, then ahead again.

"Ariana's right!" said Mattie.

"Ariana's always doing this," Mattie explained to Treeka.

"It's like her superpower—the girl sees things nobody else sees." Sandia and Evelyn nodded in agreement.

Ariana blushed. "Heh... pfft... I guess that's what happens when you draw and take pictures of everything you see since you were, like, a baby," she said with a shrug.

"I don't get it," said Treeka. "What does it mean?"

"Well," said Ariana cautiously, "I have an idea—I mean, a *hypothesis*," she said, flashing her eyebrows at Sandia.

Sandia let out a little squeal, then shook her fists in excitement.

"If we're in—*what I think we're in...*" Ariana said, looking directly at Mattie, as though speaking in code, "then the curve should continue to get tighter and tighter, in a predictable way, until we reach, what?..." she paused, waiting for Mattie to answer.

"The soft, chewy center?" asked Evelyn.

Treeka snorted.

"Almost. Sort of..." said Ariana.

"I know what you're saying," said Mattie. "I just can't believe it. It doesn't make any sense. Why would anybody build *one of those? Especially down here? And in the woods?*"

"*One of what?!*" asked Sandia. "What are you guys talking about?"

"What Ariana is trying to say," Mattie continued, "is that we are walking right into the center of a..." then Mattie stopped and interrupted herself, turning back to Ariana.

"No, it can't be..." Mattie continued as she shook her head in confusion.

"My money is on sloppy construction." Mattie said, reluctantly.

"I think we're in what was supposed to be a circle, but somebody got careless when excavating, or had a bad blueprint, or maybe had to avoid a huge boulder or something, so they altered course a little."

"WHAT ARE YOU GUYS TALKING ABOUT?!" shouted Sandia.

"Sandia..." said Ariana. Then she spoke the next words very slowly, using her "calm" voice. "What really famous design—you see them everywhere—gets bigger and bigger as you go around?"

Sandia gasped.

"I've got it!" Sandia gasped, frozen with excitement.

"A cyclotron! We're in a giant cyclotron! Wait... is that safe? Who cares! We're in a cyclotron!" Sandia squealed in excitement.

"What's a cyclotron?" Treeka asked Evelyn, quietly.

"No idea. Some physics thing," said Evelyn.

"A cyclotron is a particle accelerator that speeds particles to almost the speed of light outwards in a spiral trajectory!" Sandia said, beside herself with excitement.

"Um, no," Ariana grimaced.

"No what?" asked Sandia.

"We're not in one of those," said Ariana.

Sandia frowned and looked at Mattie.

"Nope," said Mattie.

"Then what?" asked Sandia, sounding a bit deflated.

"A golden spiral!" Ariana cooed with delight. "Nature's grand design."

"The Mother of All Mathematical Sequences," Mattie sighed.

"Fibonacci?!" cried Sandia.

Fibbo barked when he heard his name.

"Not you, Fibbo. The original one," Mattie giggled. "Fibonacci was a thirteenth century Italian mathematician," Mattie explained to the other girls.

"I've heard of Fibonacci!" said Sandia.

"Fibonacci discovered a sequence of numbers," said Ariana. "If you graph them as a series of rectangles on graph paper, it creates a very special spiral shape. This shape exists all over in nature, from the nautilus shell, to leaves on plants, even the shape of the human ear."

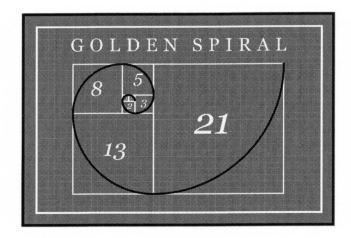

"And even the shapes of GALAXIES!" swooned Sandia. "I just love galaxies. They're so beautiful."

"That's just it, Sandia," Ariana continued. "Almost *everything* based on the golden ratio is beautiful. It's as though our brains are wired to like it."

"Renaissance painters figured this out and worked these shapes into their masterpieces," Ariana continued. "Ever since then, artists, architects, photographers, and filmmakers have been using the trick to make stuff that people like to look at."

"Soooo... we're in a spiral," Treeka said. "Cool."

"Not just any spiral, a *golden spiral!*" Ariana corrected.

"Okay, a golden spiral," said Evelyn. "Why is that important?"

Ariana thought for a moment. "I'm not exactly sure."

"This tunnel is man-made, and at great expense. Its shape is not random. It's intentional," Ariana added. "There's a saying in design that *form follows function.*

It means that structures are made not just to be pretty, but to do something. The question is, *'What?'*"

"Defense!" shouted Evelyn.

The others looked at her quizzically.

"Castles, fortresses, and bunkers," Evelyn continued, "have very special designs to make them hard to attack. Form follows function. *I get it!* Maybe this spiral tunnel is some kind of defense against invaders!"

"Or maybe it's a puzzle," suggested Treeka. "Some kind of test."

"Well one thing's for sure," said Mattie. "If it's a spiral, it will end at the center. I say we keep going, all the way to the center. By counting our steps and checking a compass, we can confirm along the way whether it's truly a golden spiral, and not just any old spiral."

"To the center!" cheered Ariana.

Fibbo barked enthusiastically. Nobody wanted to turn back now, least of all, a dog named after the discoverer of the golden spiral!

11

BY THE NUMBERS

The girls and Fibbo continued walking in the darkness of the tunnel, which continued to curve to the right.

"How do we confirm whether or not this tunnel is a golden spiral?" Sandia asked Mattie.

"It's easy—I'll show you!" said Mattie. "Evelyn, do you have any graph paper on you?"

"Is the tensile strength of aluminum forty-five thousand PSI?" replied Evelyn.

She pulled a pad of graph paper out of her pack. "For when inspiration hits," she winked at Treeka.

"Thanks," said Mattie, taking the pad. She set the pad on the ground and started to draw. "First, I'll draw a golden spiral. Then, we'll count our steps to see if the shape of this tunnel matches the shape of the spiral that I draw."

"Drawing the spiral is easy. You just make a series of squares, like this," said Mattie, as she began drawing.

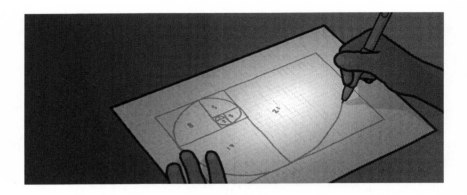

"It's such a beautiful shape!" said Sandia. "How do we know if this tunnel matches it? All we can see is one little piece of the tunnel at a time."

"Easy peasy," said Mattie. "Each section of the spiral is at 90 degrees to the last.

Evelyn, do you still have a compass on your multi-tool?"

"You bet!" said Evelyn. She carried her multi-tool whenever possible, in case she needed to repair something. It's like a Swiss army knife with pliers and other gadgets attached. One of the gadgets was a compass.

"Great," said Mattie. "You can confirm my readings. I've also got a compass app on my smart watch."

"We're currently headed due north," said Mattie. "As we walk forward in the tunnel, we'll count our steps until the compass shows we're headed due east."

The girls continued walking down the tunnel, which continued curving to the right. They counted their steps out loud as they went. Mattie kept an eye on her watch's compass while Evelyn did the same with her multi-tool.

"... 84, 85, 86..." the girls counted.

"Aaaand... stop!" said Mattie and Evelyn, at the same time. "We're now headed east," said Evelyn.

Mattie squatted down and made notes on the spiral drawing and did a few quick calculations on her watch.

"Our eighty-six steps is a quarter of the circumference of a circle," said Mattie.

"Multiply by four and we get a circle with a circumference of 344 steps, which works out to..." she tapped numbers into her watch, "... a radius of about 55 steps."

Mattie did a few more quick calculations. "If this tunnel is a true golden spiral, then it should take us about 214 steps to turn 90 degrees, heading due south.

"Great hypothesis!" said Sandia. "It's easy to test."

"If it is a golden spiral, how long until we get to the center?" Treeka asked.

"That's a good question," said Mattie. "It would take me a few minutes to calculate it. In theory, golden spirals go forever if you keep zooming in, smaller than atoms even. But this tunnel isn't actually a line, it's a ten foot wide tube. If it keeps spiraling inward, at some point, it would run into itself."

Mattie did a few more calculations. "I estimate about another 450 steps to the center," she said. "We're not very far."

"Let's keep going!" said Ariana. The others agreed and Fibbo barked.

They continued forward, counting their steps and watching the compasses.

"... 212, 213, 214 ..." the girls counted.

"Aaaand stop," said Mattie and Evelyn. "We're now facing due south!" exclaimed Evelyn. "The curve is definitely much tighter. I can see the difference now."

"We ARE in a golden spiral!" said Mattie. "Mystery solved."

"More like *mystery just begun!*" said Treeka. "Who builds crazy, mile-wide math spirals underground?"

"A—li—ens," whispered Sandia.

"There's only one way to find out," said Mattie. Let's keep going. It's not much farther now.

The tunnel kept curving to the right, but much more sharply than before.

Suddenly, the girls rounded the final bend and the tunnel opened into a circular chamber with some kind of control panel in the center.

"What the...?" said Sandia. The girls approached the control panel and shined their lights on it.

The panel contained a row of ten number dials, all set to zero. To the left of the row was a zero. To the right was a single button with an emblem in the shape of a nautilus shell.

"What do you think it means?" asked Sandia.

"It means your aliens use Arabic numerals," said Evelyn with a grin.

"It looks like a combination, like on a lock," said Ariana.

"I knew it was a puzzle!" said Treeka. "What could be the answer? It would take us forever to try every possible combination of numbers.

"Not forever, but longer than we've got," said Mattie. "Which reminds me... how long have we been gone? My parents are going to be waking up soon and they won't have any idea where we are. I'd text them to let them know we're ok, but I don't have any signal down here."

"We can head back soon," said Sandia. "I'm pretty sure they'll understand when they learn we discovered an *underground alien civilization*."

"... who uses Arabic numerals," added Evelyn.

"Should we try a combination?" asked Treeka.

"What if we get it wrong and the room fills with—I dunno, lava or something, you know... undesirable," said Evelyn.

"Lava would be awesome," said Treeka.

"There hasn't been any significant volcanic or seismic activity in these parts for thousands of years," said Sandia.

"What about snakes? Or spiders?" asked Evelyn.

"Poison gas!" said Treeka.

"Or the ceiling collapses!" said Ariana, very pleased to have thought of something equally terrible.

"I don't think we need to guess the combination," said Mattie. "I think I know what it is. At least, I have a pretty decent guess."

"How?" asked Sandia. "There are just a bunch of numbers. The combination could be anything."

"I don't think it's just any random number," said Mattie. "I think Treeka is right—I think it's a puzzle."

"This whole tunnel is a clue, and so is the button with the nautilus design—an obvious reference to Fibonacci. As Sandia mentioned, this shell is probably the most famous example of the Fibonacci series."

"And the last clue," Mattie continued, "is this zero to the left of the dials. Why would the people who built this include that?"

The girls shrugged. "No idea," said Evelyn.

"Mathematicians sometimes debate about whether the Fibonacci series starts with zero or one," Mattie explained. "By showing the zero, they're telling us where to start."

"The Fibonacci series!" cried Ariana.

"Yes!" said Mattie.

The girls all looked at each other, barely able to contain their excitement.

"What do you say? Should we try it?" asked Mattie. "Anybody who would rather leave, I understand. You know, snakes or whatever."

"Poison gas," said Treeka.

"Poison gas," said Mattie. "Whatever happens. Who's in?"

"I'm in!" Sandia cried.

"Me too," said Treeka.

"Yes!" said Ariana and Evelyn.

"Ok, we're all in then," said Ariana. "Mattie, do you know the numbers in the Fibonacci series?"

"Easy peasy," said Mattie. "We've got it right here," she said, holding up the graph paper with the golden spiral. "It's simply the length of each of these boxes: 1, 1, 2, 3, 5, 8, 13, 21. Look! There's room to enter exactly ten digits into the combination."

"Here goes," said Mattie. She entered the numbers into the number dials.

Nothing happened.

"Now what?" asked Sandia.

"Press the shell button," said Treeka. They all looked at each other and agreed.

Just as Mattie was about to press the button, Ariana snapped a picture, startling everyone. "Sorry," she said, smiling.

Mattie pressed the nautilus button. It depressed with a click sound.

All was silent. The girls looked at one another, not sure what to do next.

Just then, they heard a low rumbling sound. The floor of the circular chamber in which they stood started to move.

12

THE NAUTILUS SOCIETY

"The floor is lowering!" cried Mattie. Fibbo started barking.

"It's an elevator!" said Evelyn.

They all shined their flashlights all around as they descended into a much larger room.

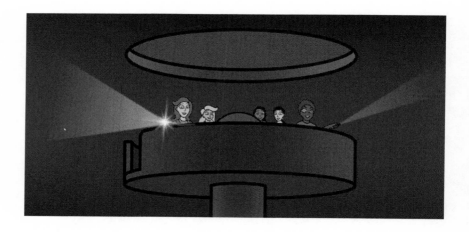

After a few seconds, the floor came to a halt at the bottom of the room and the low rumbling sound stopped. All was quiet. Nobody said anything. Even Fibbo was quiet.

In the beam of the girls' flashlights, they saw what appeared to be tables, chairs, and lots of shelves.

"A light!" said Ariana, pointing. "There, on that wall."

They all looked at the wall. There was a small switch emitting a faint glow. Slowly, the girls made their way to the switch.

"What *IS* this place?" asked Sandia.

The girls arrived at the glowing switch. It was labeled "ON" and "OFF."

"A light switch?" wondered Mattie out loud.

The girls all looked at one another, as though wondering who should flip the switch.

"I'll do it," said Treeka. She reached up and flipped the switch.

Somewhere in the distance, a gentle hum could be heard. The girls felt a slight breeze, and then smelled the air change from musty to fresh, like a window had been opened. And then, one by one, dozens of lights began to turn on.

For the first time, the girls could see the massive room around them. It had a high, domed ceiling made of interesting shapes, with large paintings and photographs of people.

In the center of the ceiling was a round hole, the one through which they had entered on the elevator. All around the walls were several doors and row after row of shelves filled with books and several large machines the size of refrigerators.

"It looks like a library," said Sandia. "And look up there on the ceiling... Galileo, Copernicus, Marie Curie..."

"Lady Ada Lovelace," said Treeka, pointing at one of the faces. "The first computer programmer."

"Da Vinci, the Wright Brothers, and Beulah Louise Henry—also known as Lady Edison," said Evelyn, looking all around at the faces above.

"Michelangelo, Rembrandt, Van Gogh, and—wow!—St. Catherine of Bologna," Ariana cooed.

"Euclid, Descarte, Isaac Newton, and Emmy Noether..." said Mattie.

Ariana walked over to one of the chairs. She swiped her finger along the top. It was covered with a fine layer of dust.

"Look here," she said. "Letters are stenciled onto the back of this chair. 'PROPERTY OF U.S. DEPT OF WAR.'"

"Note to self: Don't take that chair," joked Treeka.

"I'm starting to think maybe we're not supposed to be down here," said Sandia.

"I don't think anyone's been here for a long time," replied Mattie. "It looks like whoever built it has forgotten that it exists."

"Be right back, gonna go find the Lost Ark in a crate," chuckled Treeka.

"Your time frame is right on, Treeka," said Evelyn.

"In 1947, the War Department changed its name when it split into the Departments of the Army and Air Force. In 1949, they all became the Department of Defense, which is what they still call it today."

"Who needs a library when you've got an Evelyn!" said Ariana.

Evelyn winked at her.

The girls drifted apart as they explored the fascinating room, mostly in silence, as though they had discovered some kind of special place that deserved respect and reverence.

Treeka broke the silence with a gasp. "Holy moly! Come look at this you guys!" she said.

On the wall in front of Treeka was a map depicting a massive structure built into a mountain. In the center was an arrow that said "you are here."

"This is just one room, a library" said Treeka. "It's part of something much bigger!"

"A military base?" asked Sandia.

"No, I don't think so," said Evelyn. "More like a command center. Or maybe a doomsday shelter."

"What's a doomsday shelter?" asked Ariana.

"It's something people take shelter in when something bad is happening outside, like a war," said Evelyn.

"Or an ecological disaster," said Sandia.

"Or a zombie apocalypse!" cheered Treeka.

"I'm not sure this is funny," said Mattie. "Whoever built this place was serious. I think we need to keep looking for clues."

At this, Sandia instinctively whipped out her magnifying glass.

"The map shows many levels," said Treeka. "Living quarters, recreation, kitchen, machine shop, laboratory, storage, facilities. Look here, we are standing in the library."

"Here's the entrance where we came in, at the top of the library," said Mattie.

There are other tunnels, too. I wonder where they come out."

"This place is awesome," Ariana whispered in amazement.

"Literally," agreed Evelyn.

"I don't understand how something so large could be kept a secret. Or forgotten," said Sandia. "Curious indeed!"

"We could explore this place for days!" said Treeka.

"Yes, we could," said Mattie. "But we should come back later. I don't want to worry my parents, so we should start heading back."

"Just one thing," said Ariana. "According to the map, through that archway is something called the 'Great Hall.' Maybe we could take a peek before we go."

Sandia grinned, nodding her head in agreement.

Everyone looked at Mattie. She nodded. "Okay. Just a few more minutes though.

We really do need to get back."

They made their way past several large bookshelves and down a hallway, where they opened a pair of large, red doors into the chamber labeled "Great Hall" on the map.

The Great Hall was an auditorium. It was shaped like the library and had enough seats for about 250 people.

At the front of the auditorium was a stage with a lectern, a statue, and a desk.

The girls quietly walked down the ramp in a single file to the front of the auditorium and climbed up onto the stage.

As they walked closer to the desk, they noticed that there was some kind of machine and an old-fashioned telephone resting on it. They looked as if they'd hadn't been used for many, many years.

"Wow," said Treeka. "An old rotary phone." My grandparents had one of those in their garage.

"What's that machine?" Ariana wondered aloud but not to anyone in particular.

"Hey, check this out!" announced Mattie. "That's Isaac Newton!" exclaimed Mattie, pointing at the statue.

"He discovered the laws of optics, and the laws of motion, and the laws of gravity. And along the way, he *invented* calculus!" she continued.

"And then he turned twenty-six!" said Sandia, quoting one of her favorite scientists, Neil deGrasse Tyson.

Mattie giggled.

"Whoa..." said Treeka, examining the statue closely.

"Look at the ring on his finger!" exclaimed Ariana.

The others leaned closer, scanning the statue's hands for clues.

They all spotted it at the same time: On the left index finger of the Isaac Newton statue was a ring in the shape of the nautilus shell.

"There it is again!" said Mattie. "That shell. It keeps showing up in this place. What does it mean?"

"That is certainly the question of the day," Treeka replied.

"The emblem is over here, too," said Evelyn, pointing at a glowing button on the console of the machine.

The button looked just like the button the girls had pressed to lower the elevator at the Fibonacci combination.

Evelyn paused, glanced over to the others, then pressed the button.

The machine started whirring, and the girls could hear the hissing sound of an old-time recording through speakers far overhead in the chamber's ceiling.

A recorded voice began to speak. They all froze.

"Ladies and gentlemen, esteemed members of the Nautilus Society, thank you for coming to the Shell Mountain research and knowledge vault facility."

The girls all looked at each other.

"As you know," the recorded voice continued, *"there have been times in human history when the darkness of fear and ignorance covered the earth, forcing the light of knowledge, education, art, science, and enlightened thinking to go into hiding, to go underground to ride out the storm, until a time when knowledge can emerge and once again enlighten the world."*

"We fear that such a dark time may be upon us now. As a precaution, we have designed this top secret Shell Mountain facility to exist as a safe place for research, scholarship, and the preservation of the world's knowledge."

The machine stopped, and the room was once again silent. No one said a word for several seconds as they tried to absorb what they had heard.

"I don't understand," said Sandia. "Where did the people go?"

"And who were they?" Evelyn inquired.

"Did anyone recognize the voice?" Ariana asked.

They all shook their heads in unison, then they continued to investigate the large room.

"Look here," said Evelyn. "The phone. It has the nautilus shell on it. And a sign: In case of emergency, dial 1-1-2-3-5-8."

"The Fibonacci series again!" exclaimed Mattie.

The girls all stopped talking, unsure what to do next. They were all thinking the same thing.

"Should we..." said Treeka, unsure of herself, "try calling... the number?"

"But this isn't an emergency," said Mattie.

"Oh, I disagree!" said Sandia. "The world is facing all kinds of emergencies! Climate change, mass extinction of species, ocean acidification... and I've gotta say, there are many signs that fear and ignorance are spreading, and lots of people who are ignoring—or who don't understand—science."

"I'm guessing the top-secret shell people already know all that," said Treeka. "They don't need us to tell them if they just watch the news."

"Besides, this phone is like, 60 or 70 years old," said Evelyn. "I doubt it even works."

"Everything else works—the lights, and the recorded voice, and the elevator and stuff," said Ariana. "Why wouldn't the phone?"

"True..." said Evelyn. "But, who would still be around to answer it?"

"I can think of an easy way to find out," said Treeka impishly, wiggling her fingers above the telephone receiver.

"I don't know," said Mattie. "We might get in trouble. I don't think we're supposed to be down here."

"I don't know," said Ariana. "Look around... this place almost seems like it was MADE for us. People who love science and learning. I feel kind of magical just being down here in this special place."

"Ariana is right," said Treeka. "This place rocks." She thought for a moment. "I've got it! Let's just pick up the phone, for just a second, and listen to hear if there's a dial tone. Then we can hang up. We don't have to call the shell number, but we'd know if it's working."

The girls pondered this.

"It would tell us a lot more about the phone than we know now," said Sandia.

The others nodded. As though by silent agreement, everyone looked at Treeka. It had been her idea, after all.

"Okay," said Treeka. She slowly lifted the phone and put it up to her ear. She let out a gasp.

13

STEAMTEAM 5: THE BEGINNING

"What is it?" asked Sandia.

"It's a dial tone," replied Treeka. "The phone still works!"

"Hang up!" said Mattie. The others nodded fast.

Treeka quickly hung up the phone and took a step back.

"What do we do now?" asked Ariana.

"We go home, that's what we do," said Mattie.

The others agreed. They walked back to the circular elevator platform and pushed the button. It raised them up to the ceiling and into the tunnel through which they had entered the complex.

ONCE THEY WERE BACK IN THE TUNNEL, THE GIRLS WALKED silently for a long time, deep in thought. Fibbo trotted alongside them, happy to be walking again.

At last, Treeka spoke. "I've been thinking about it," she said. "I think we should keep this place a secret. For now, at least."

"But don't you think the world has a right to know?" asked Sandia. "I mean, all of those books. Who knows what treasures might be in there."

"They belong in a museum!" quipped Evelyn.

"It kind of *is* a museum!" said Ariana, cheerfully.

"I think Treeka's right," said Mattie. "We don't really know what we're dealing with yet. We have a lot more to learn about it. And we can always tell the world later, and maybe find a way to protect it. But once the secret is out, we can never undo it. The cautious thing to do would be to keep it to ourselves for now."

THE GIRLS ARRIVED AT THE LADDER WHERE THEY HAD FIRST entered the tunnel. Sunshine beamed in from above. They climbed up one by one, and carefully lifted Fibbo up to the woods above.

"Consider yourself rescued," Mattie said to Fibbo, who wagged his tail with appreciation.

Evelyn retrieved her electric skateboard and helmet, while Treeka inspected Drone. "A nice recharge of the battery and he'll be good as new!" she said.

They began walking home.

Sandia thought for a moment. "What do we tell our parents?" she asked. "We can't lie to them."

"It wouldn't be a lie if we told them we have a clubhouse in the woods," suggested Ariana. "I mean, assuming we used the secret underground complex *as* a clubhouse."

"Oh yeaahh!" said Treeka. "The clubhouse to end all clubhouses. The King of the World of clubhouses."

"All we need now is a club," said Mattie.

"Well one thing's for sure," said Ariana, "we sure do work well together."

The girls agreed. "We do make a great team!" said Sandia, as they emerged from the trees. Mattie's backyard was just ahead.

Seeing the tent they had slept in the night before reminded Evelyn of the fun night they had had. She looked down at her friendship bracelet that Ariana had made.

S-T-E-A-M, the letters read.

"*STEAMTEAM 5!*" shouted Evelyn, holding up her bracelet for the others to see.

They all looked at their bracelets, too.

"*I love it!*" said Mattie.

"Evelyn always adds a number when she names her inventions," Ariana told Treeka.

"Makes it snazzy," said Evelyn.

"All in favor of STEAMTEAM 5, say *aye*," said Sandia.

"Aye!" shouted the girls. It was unanimous. Even Fibbo barked his approval.

SOMEWHERE FAR AWAY, A YOUNG MAN IN A WELL-TAILORED SUIT entered a dark room with giant screens all over the walls. The screens showed maps, charts, satellite images, and television news channels in many languages from around the world.

The silhouette of a figure sat in front of the screens, watching intently.

"Excuse me, Madam Director," said the man to the silhouette.

"Yes, Anton?" said the figure.

"One of the Nautilus sites has been activated. In North America," said Anton.

"Interesting," said the figure. "Please close the door, and tell me the details."

THE END

SANDIA, TREEKA, EVELYN, ARIANA, AND MATTIE RETURN IN:

STEAMTEAM 5 Book 2: Mystery at Makerspace

FREE EBOOK

To receive a free .PDF of *STEAMTeam 5 Chronicles: Mystery of the Haunted Cider Mill*, send an email to:

info@steamteam5.com

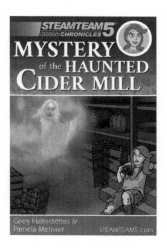

Made in the USA
Coppell, TX
14 December 2019